# The Lion Keeper

Written by Sandra Agard

Illustrated by Anthony Ikediuba

**Collins**

# 1 Introduction – They called him Boy

His name was Adewale, but they tried to take that away from him. They tried to take his name, a name given to him by his parents, after they took him from his homeland. They gave him a new name: they called him Boy.

The raiders had come during the night. His family had been woken roughly with screams and shouts, the breaking and ripping of his home. He watched as his village was burnt to the ground. His arms and legs were bound tightly to another boy, Ola.

Ola was older than him. The boys had said nothing to
each other – there was nothing to say. They were marched
away from where their village had once stood. It was
the beginning of the long journey to the coast. They were
marched through forests and across rivers, miles and miles,
leaving behind everything that was familiar.

When they reached the coast, Adewale was separated
from Ola and forced into the darkness of a cell. He was
surrounded by people crying, chained and terrified. He was
so far away from home. Everything was new and he was
so afraid. What had happened to Ola, his own family,
their village? Would he ever see them again?

Eventually, they forced him onto a vessel they called a ship. It was on the ship that they began calling him Boy. They called him Boy as they took away his language, as they forced him to learn their tongue – English – so that he could follow their commands. They were cruel and had no patience, so he had to learn fast.

They called him Boy now in this place called the Tower
of London – his strange new home in the grey land they
call England.

He was not Boy! He wouldn't forget the name his parents
gave to him – that was his promise to himself. It was the only
thing he had to remind himself of what he'd lost – it was
his secret. He wouldn't let it go. His name was Adewale.

# 2 A frosty day

The Tower of London had been many things – a palace, an armoury, a treasury and a prison. Standing tall and proud on the banks of the River Thames, it was also the home of the Royal Menagerie, full of animals from around the world. Adewale now shared their fate, trapped within the walls of the stone tower.

The bells of the nearby church, All Hallows by the Tower, rang out, waking up the day. London was already busy, horse-drawn carriages travelled back and forth taking bankers and merchants to morning meetings in coffee houses. Markets were busy with people eager to buy meat and fish – even the new fruits of bananas and pineapples that were proving popular.

The docks on the River Thames never slept. Ships from all over the world were constantly sailing through bringing all kinds of goods to London. Snow had fallen heavily during the night, covering the Tower of London in a blanket of ice and frost. It was bitterly cold, but nothing would stop the day's work. The Yeomen Warders, who guarded the Tower, were making the final preparations for the morning's customers. The gates would be opened soon, and the crowds would be let in, eager to see the wide variety of exotic animals kept in the Royal Menagerie, especially the lions and the polar bear.

Adewale had been amazed at the sight of snow falling from the sky. He'd never seen anything like it. The way it crept so quietly over everything was strange and frightening. The first time he touched it, he was shocked at the icy sting it left on his fingers. Adewale's home across the big sea was one of sun and warmth. He tried not to think about his homeland and his lost family; it hurt too much. He couldn't help it, but he longed to return. At home, only rain fell from the sky. It was cooling. The rains would refresh the land, preparing it for the crops his family and village would plant. This was the opposite: the brutal cold that fell wouldn't leave. He didn't like the cold and neither did the lions. They spent the majority of their time lying in their den at the edge of the pit trying to stay warm, and often had to be coaxed with food into the centre so they could be seen by the paying crowds.

The pit was located in what was known as the Lion
Tower at the far end of the main courtyard. On the other
side of the courtyard was the polar bear which seemed to
enjoy the cold. Adewale had heard that it came from a land
of snow.

"Roarrrrr!" A deep rumbling was heard from a dark
corner of the pit.

Adewale looked towards the sound. The lions were
waking up. He had to hurry. Even though he wasn't as
afraid of them as when he'd first started caring for them in
the spring, they still scared him a little.

Adewale had been up since first light cleaning out the pit. This had been one of his main jobs since arriving at the Tower of London. He always tried to do it quickly and keep as far away from the lions as he possibly could. This morning, he'd swept out the old straw and replaced it with new straw. He'd filled up the pails with fresh water and cleared out the feeding baskets. Now he would fill the baskets with new food. The scraps from Cook's kitchen would be breakfast today.

The lions didn't like the food; they never ate much. Adewale didn't like it either. In fact, he didn't like anything about his new home.

He tried not to think of his lost family, his lost home, but memories would come flooding back. How he missed his mother's pounded yam, the fish caught with his father, and playing with his brothers and sisters around the beautiful baobab tree that grew in the middle of the village. This had also been the place where the whole village had gathered to listen to stories and share special moments. They were such happy days, now to be replaced by this strange land and people he didn't understand at all. Everything was so different here. The food. The clothes. The weather. The words. The manners. The name they called him. He'd learnt quickly for he had no choice if he wanted to survive this new world.

# 3 Mr Jacks

"Boy!" The deep booming voice of Mr Jacks echoed across the courtyard. Mr Jacks was the Master in Charge of the Royal Menagerie. He had a vicious temper, especially if he felt things weren't exactly the way he wanted them, so Adewale needed to finish all of his tasks quickly if he didn't want to feel the pain of Mr Jacks's boot.

He was a cruel, unforgiving man. Adewale had so few things to be grateful for but learning English on the ship that brought him here was one of them. It had served him well and saved him a lot of pain. Mr Jacks didn't like to repeat himself – not understanding could lead to a swift beating.

"Boy! Where are you?" the voice came again. It was closer now. It still stung, being called Boy. He hated it. He'd tried to tell people his real name, but they refused to listen and sometimes he would receive a swift boot or a whack with the rod for speaking.

Adewale climbed out of the pit and was heading for the door, but his way out was suddenly blocked by the large figure of Mr Jacks.

He was a tall man with long brown hair and an untidy brown beard. His hands were large with strong, long fingers and broken nails. They were covered with old scars from his many years at sea.

Mr Jacks was never in a good mood but today he seemed even angrier than usual.

"Didn't you hear me calling you?" Mr Jacks yelled.

"The lions – " began Adewale, his voice barely a whisper.

"What about them?" snapped Mr Jacks.

"I was still in the pit. They were just waking up and I didn't want to upset them, Mr Jacks," said Adewale quietly.

Mr Jacks shot Adewale a disgusted look before continuing: "You've been daydreaming again, more likely. Don't get behind with your work, Boy! Or you'll feel my boot!"

Adewale's heart began to beat faster. He often felt
Mr Jacks' boot and was keen to avoid it if he could.

"The gates are opening at 12 o'clock sharp!" continued
Mr Jacks. "The crowds will be in to see our lions, Samson
and Cleo, and YOU!"

"Me – ?" whispered Adewale, beginning to tremble.
He didn't like the way Mr Jacks was looking at him.

"Yes, you Boy. We're going to give the crowds
a show! We're going to give them the African Prince,
the Lion Keeper!" Mr Jacks laughed.

15

Adewale couldn't believe his ears. He was going to be in the show with the lions! Looking after them from a safe distance was one thing, but to be in there when they were running around – this couldn't be happening to him. He began to shake even more. "But, Sir, what … what am I going to do with them?" Adewale asked.

"I just told you. Put on a show, entertain the crowd," said Mr Jacks, waving his hands in the air.

"But how?" asked Adewale.

"You'll find a way! You lived in the jungle, didn't you? You must have dealt with plenty of beasts in your time! Oh! What a show you'll put on, Boy. It'll be the best show in London. Now, I'll have no more lip from you! My decision is final, and you'll do as you're told! I paid good money for you!"

Mr Jacks snarled, raising one of his large hands menacingly. "Now get out of my sight! I'll call you when it's time!"

# 4 The dream

Adewale ran past Mr Jacks, eager to avoid another beating. As he crossed the icy courtyard, he saw a large bird sitting on a wall looking at him. Cook had called it a raven.

Its dark, sharp eyes seemed to stare right through him. It was carrying something in its claw. It spread its wings and flew up into the sky towards what was known as the White Tower. Adewale wished he could fly away like that, then maybe he could fly home.

Cook had told him a story. It was said that if the ravens ever left the Tower, the kingdom of England would fall; it would be doomed. It made these mysterious birds seem almost magical and once again he was reminded of home, of the stories his grandparents would tell him of special birds and their adventures in the sky.

His favourite story was the story about the hunter and the sunbird. The hunter had gone into the forest to try and catch the sunbird and win great glory. But the hunter got lost and he feared he would never find his way home. After many hours, he finally found the sunbird, but he changed his mind about catching it and let it fly away. In return for his kindness, the sunbird led him out of the forest back to his village.

Adewale wished that a sunbird could arrive to lead him home from this terrible place.

He returned to his quarters and fell onto his bedding. He was very tired. Despite knowing that he could get in trouble for sleeping during the day, he fell asleep anyway and began to dream. His dreams always took him back to his village and that fateful night when he was taken away from everybody he'd loved.

Adewale dreamt he was walking through the remains of his village which had been burnt to the ground that night the raiders had come.

He was calling for his family. Usually there was only silence. But this time it was different. He heard the beat of his grandfather's djembe, a drum he would use when telling stories to the whole village. His grandfather was the griot who kept all the stories and histories of the village. His grandparents were standing near the ashes of his home. They were smiling, but as he approached, they began to fade away.

"What should I do?" Adewale cried, tears rolling down his face.

"Come home," was his grandmother's response.

"But how? I'm so far away," he cried. He tried to reach for them, but they disappeared. The sound of the drum lingered but eventually that too faded.

Adewale sat up. He knew now more than ever that he had to escape and somehow return home.

Nobody was going to stop him. Not even Mr Jacks!

# 5 The plan

This wasn't the first time Adewale had thought about running away. He'd wanted to escape from the beginning. He'd even come up with a plan.

Mr Jacks would go to the docks with Adewale to collect goods, such as tea, sugar and chocolate, which Adewale would carry. On these trips, he'd see ships much like the one that brought him to this land, and he'd overhear sailors talking about travelling to Africa and to the Gold Coast.

Adewale remembered that name. The Gold Coast was what they called it, the place where he'd boarded the ship that brought him here. If he could get back there, he could find his way home. Although he'd walked for many days before getting on the ship, he felt if he could just get back to the place called the Gold Coast, it would be the start of finding his way back home.

He didn't want to think what might await him. He just wanted to get home. One of those ships could take him there – he knew it. However, this plan always felt like a dream. How was he going to get on one of those ships? How would he find the right one to take him home? It felt too dangerous – too impossible – until exactly four days ago when a chance encounter gave him the opportunity he craved.

On that day, whilst waiting for Mr Jacks on the quayside, he'd recognised the language of his homeland. His heart had leapt for joy. He turned around and saw two African men lifting barrels. They wore long heavy coats, and their heads were wrapped in cloth. For the first time in a long time, he had a smile on his face and some joy in his heart.

He'd been told not to move by Mr Jacks, but hearing those voices brought back so many memories and feelings. He forgot all about Mr Jacks and rushed over to them.

The taller of the two looked at the small boy and smiled. Adewale smiled back and they gestured to him to come nearer. They crouched behind some huge rolls of cotton and began to whisper in the language he thought he'd never hear again. They told him he'd need money but if he could find them again, they could help him get home.

People who worked at the Tower and people who sold goods to Mr Jacks got metal coins. It reminded Adewale of the cowrie shells people would use to trade back home.

Mr Jacks always had lots of coins after a show at the Lion Tower, but he never gave Adewale any money like he gave everyone else. Mr Jacks would take the coins into his room. If Adewale got a chance, just one moment when Mr Jacks wasn't looking, then maybe, just maybe, he could grab some money and get away – after all, he was owed something for all the work he'd done since arriving at the Tower.

He knew it had been four days since he'd met the sailors because he'd scratched a mark for each sunrise since then into the floor of his quarters. He also knew this meant that the sailors would be leaving for Africa tomorrow morning.

For days, the plan had tossed in his mind. He didn't know if he would have the courage to go through with it. The truth was he was afraid. Afraid of what would happen if he tried and failed. Severe beatings, maybe worse … But after seeing his grandparents in that dream … after being called home, he had to try. He might not get another chance. He had to run, and he had to do it tonight.

# 6 The lion show

The church bells chimed: it was 12 o'clock. The gates of the Tower of London swung open, and a large crowd of people rushed in. Word had spread that for the first time the African boy would be part of the lion show. Some were there to see if an African really could command wild animals; others to see if he would be eaten.

Mr Jacks stepped forward to face the crowd. He raised his hands to silence them.

"Good morning, ladies and gentlemen! Welcome to the Tower of London. There are many fine creatures from all corners of the world for you to see. There's something for everyone – "

"We want to see the lions!" someone shouted from the crowd.

"And lions you will see, my friend. We've the best show in London for you today. All the way from darkest Africa … I give you the African Prince. The Lion Tamer!"

The crowd clapped and yelled.

The lions started roaring at the sudden loud noises.

"Boy!" hissed Mr Jacks. "Get on with the show. These people have paid good money!"

Adewale placed food in the middle of the pit. This was usually the part where he would leave but he could feel Mr Jacks' steely gaze on him – this time he wasn't going anywhere. Adewale's heart began to beat faster. Sweat ran down his forehead. He could hardly breathe. He must stay calm … he must!

The lions, Samson and Cleo, came out of their dens. Adewale hoped that they would eat the food and fall asleep as they usually did. Hopefully, they would ignore him completely. They looked at the food and then looked at Adewale. Samson began to growl. Cleo sniffed the air and began walking slowly towards him. Samson, still growling, followed Cleo. The crowd cheered even louder.

Adewale's mouth was suddenly very dry. His heart
was now beating so loudly, he was sure everyone could
hear it. The crowd's cheers were growing louder, and some
people were even laughing. The lions got closer and closer.
He'd never been so near to them, their fangs and claws
looked enormous. What was he going to do? Then he
remembered something. He hadn't seen any lions growing
up, they had never come into the village, but his father had
still taught him what to do if he ever saw one.

"*Never run or turn your back. You must hold your ground.*" His father's words were now ringing in his head. He made himself as large as possible and clapped and waved his arms. The lions edged towards him … closer, closer … but Adewale didn't back down. The lions hesitated, then looked at him and snarled, but eventually they decided that the food on the ground was an easier meal. The lions pounced on the meat and ripped it apart. Once they finished eating, they yawned and stretched, then turned their backs on the crowd and returned to their den.

Adewale breathed a sigh of relief. Many in the crowd clapped at the display. Some booed, apparently upset that Adewale hadn't been the lions' meal.

"Well maybe they'll get him next time, folks," Mr Jacks's voice boomed throughout the courtyard.

Jacks steered the crowd towards the other animals.

Adewale was relieved that he'd survived the lion show. But he knew an even greater test awaited him. He picked up some straw and began to clean up the pit. As he worked, he knew it was nearly time for his great escape. When night fell, he would run.

# 7 Escape

The takings from the day's show had been the highest ever. So that night, Mr Jacks celebrated by having a very big dinner. He ate two delicious meat pies and a whole roasted chicken. Afterwards, he was very full and fell asleep on a chair in his room, snoring loudly. This was the chance that Adewale had been waiting for.

He waited until everyone was asleep, then he tiptoed towards Mr Jacks' room, moving as quietly as possible so he wouldn't wake anyone.

Adewale pushed open the door slowly. It creaked slightly.
He hardly dared to breathe. He looked around
the untidy room. Mr Jacks was slumped in a chair,
snoring deeply.

The pouch containing the money from the day's show
was sitting on the bed next to Mr Jacks's keys, and a big
cloak was hanging on the wall in the corner.

Adewale didn't hesitate. He grabbed the pouch and the keys and took down the cloak, wrapping himself in it. It was heavier than he expected and he stumbled, falling onto the floor. He froze.

Mr Jacks grunted and twisted in his chair, but he didn't wake up. Adewale rose and quietly crept out of the room and into the night.

There were usually two Yeomen Warders patrolling the courtyard at night. One would stay on the main gate. The other would walk around the grounds. Adewale had to time his run carefully so he wouldn't be caught. He thanked the stars that there was no full moon that night.

The Yeomen Warder passed him as he crouched in
the darkness. He wrapped the cloak tightly around him.
Once the way was clear, Adewale ran across the courtyard,
keeping to the shadows. He made it to the main gate
without being seen. He was pleased to see that the guard at
the main gate had fallen asleep. Perhaps he'd also enjoyed
a big dinner.

Adewale fumbled with the keys. He'd often seen
Mr Jacks open the gate and knew that it was the largest
key he needed. His fingers were very cold, and he had to
use all his strength to turn the key in the lock. It opened
with a loud click. Adewale looked in all directions;
nobody came. Quickly, he pushed the gate open and went
through it. He was free but not safe yet. Somehow, he'd
have to get to the docks.

He placed the keys on the ground, closed the gate and
ran swiftly into the night. He had to get away as far as
possible before anyone realised he was gone.

# 8 On the run

The Tower was behind him. Adewale closed his eyes, willing himself to remember the way, willing himself to be calm. He took a deep breath, wondering what it would be like to be free again.

In daylight, the docks hadn't seemed far from the Tower. But now everything appeared to have changed. He looked up to the sky. The moon was still hidden behind some clouds, but the stars were shining brightly; it reminded him of the sky back home. Suddenly, he was no longer afraid. He pulled the cloak tighter. He had to get away from the Tower, as far away as possible. Mr Jacks or the guard at the gate could wake up any minute.

He heard something moving towards him. Quickly, he
ducked into the darkness of a nearby alley. A horse-drawn
carriage rolled past him. He waited until the sound of
the carriage was far away, then he continued his journey.
Why did everything look so different? He was already
feeling hopeless, when his eyes caught a familiar sight
– the church they always passed as they headed toward
the docks. He was on the right path. He hurried on.

More snow had fallen that afternoon and it had
got colder. Adewale was glad about this for there were
fewer people around; they all kept to themselves.

He thought about the warmth of his homeland, and this pushed him on towards the docks.

He began to recognise familiar sights – like shops, and London Bridge, as Mr Jacks had called it. He knew he was nearly there when suddenly a voice yelled: "Oi! What you doing?"

Adewale stopped, turned around and was faced with the bright light of a flaming torch.

"You lost?" continued the voice. "For a couple of farthings, I can take you anywhere in London," the voice hastily added. "I'm the best linkboy in London town. The name's John. Where do you want to go?"

Adewale hesitated slightly but then said: "The docks."

"You aren't far away … But hey, aren't you the Lion Tamer from the Tower?"

"I … I – " began Adewale.

"So, you didn't get eaten then!" John laughed. "You going away?"

"I'm going home," replied Adewale.

John looked at him and nodded. "We all need to find a home. Follow me."

Adewale opened the pouch and handed John a shilling.

The two young boys crossed the bridge towards the docks.

He was nearly there.

# 9 Discovery

Jacks rose stiffly from the chair. His eyes immediately went to the bed. Where was the pouch? Where was the money?

He stumbled to the door and shouted: "Boy! Boy!"

He waited. Usually, the boy would come running in. Now there was only silence.

Jacks never liked to be kept waiting.

"Boy, where are you?"

He could hear footsteps.

"At last! You better have a good excuse for me having to call twice – "

But it wasn't Boy who entered the room, it was one of the Yeomen Warders.

"Mr Jacks, Sir. These were found by the gate this morning," and he handed Jacks a set of keys.

Jacks took the keys and shouted: "Where's Boy?"

"Nobody has seen him, Sir," came the reply.

"What do you mean, nobody has seen him! Have you checked the pit … the kitchen?"

"Everywhere has been searched. He's gone."

"Gone?! Gone?! What do you mean – gone? He's my property!"

"I'm sorry, Sir. We've searched everywhere. There's no sign of him. The lions were fed by Henry the stableboy. He wasn't happy!" said the Yeomen Warder.

"Fetch my cloak. I'll search myself and when I find that boy – "

"Sir, your cloak isn't here," said the Yeoman Warder.

"What?" yelled Jacks. "BOY!"

Down in the pit, Samson and Cleo began to roar.

# 10 Freedom

The two boys reached the docks just as the sun was rising over a snow-covered London.

"What ship is it?" asked John.

"I don't know," said Adewale. "I'll wait here."

"I hope you get back home," said John.

"So do I," said Adewale, and they parted.

Adewale crouched down behind the large rolls of cotton and waited. Would the two men from his home return? He could do nothing else but hope and wait.

He was suddenly very tired, his whole body ached and, despite trying not to, he fell asleep.

Adewale was woken up by someone shaking his arm.

"So, you made it, little brother. Good."

Adewale slowly opened his eyes. The sun at first dazzled his eyes and for a moment he couldn't remember where he was. Fear gripped him and then he saw the tall African man smiling down at him.

Adewale smiled back.

"We speak English from now on," said the man. "The English become uncomfortable when they don't understand what we're saying."

Adelwale rose stiffly from the bales of cotton. No more snow had fallen but it was still cold. He stretched his arms upwards. The sun was bright but gave no heat. He could never understand how this was possible. Back home in the village, it was always hot, even when the rains fell. Remembering his village made him feel happy. He was beginning his journey home. He followed the two men, but when he came to board the ship, he stopped as memories flooded back of the terrible conditions of his first sea journey. He didn't want to relive such a journey again.

"What's wrong, little brother?" asked the smaller of
the men.

"I … I'm afraid. Ships have many deaths," Adewale
said softly.

"Yes, we've heard the terrible stories of those slave ships.
This one isn't like that. We carry cargo like cotton and
tea to the Caribbean and America from here, Africa, India
and China. We work hard for our keep … our freedom.
You're small and fast, so you'll make a good cabin boy.
The captain needs one," the taller man said. "Come, we
must catch the tide before it's too late."

Adewale followed the two men onto the ship. He was put to work immediately, untying tangled ropes as the boat left the dock.

The taller of the men approached him and said: "Little brother, what was the name given to you by your family?"

"Adewale." It felt so good to say his name out loud.

"Haa … a name that means the crown is coming home, a fitting one for your journey," said the taller man.

"Yes, it is," beamed Adewale.

He paused for a moment and looked back towards the docks. In the distance, he could see the Tower of London. He could just about make out the ravens circling over its top. He thought about the lions, and it saddened him that they couldn't share in his freedom. But the much more powerful feeling within him was hope ... a feeling that grew larger as London got further and further away. As London disappeared from view, so did the name they had given him.

He was Boy no longer. His name was Adewale, and he was finally going home.

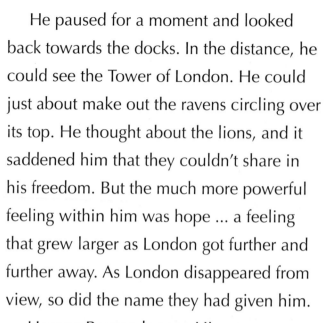

# Different lives

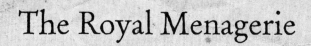

## The Royal Menagerie

*presents*

### Prince of Africa,
### Tamer of Beasts,
### the Lion Keeper

Tickets – one shilling

# Ideas for reading

Written by Gill Matthews
*Primary Literacy Consultant*

**Reading objectives:**
- check that the book makes sense to them, discussing their understanding and exploring the meaning of words in context
- ask questions to improve their understanding
- draw inferences such as inferring characters' feelings, thoughts and motives from their actions, and justify inferences with evidence

**Spoken language objectives:**
- articulate and justify answers, arguments and opinions
- participate in discussions, presentations, performances, role play, improvisations and debates
- select and use appropriate registers for effective communication

**Curriculum links:** History – a study of an aspect or theme in British history that extends pupils' chronological knowledge beyond 1066

**Interest words:** palace, armoury, treasury, prison, menagerie

**Resources:** IT

## Build a context for reading

- Ask children to explore the covers of the book. Discuss what they expect the story to be about.
- Read the first three sentences of the back-cover blurb. Ask children who they think 'they' are. Discuss how someone can take a home and a name.
- Ask children what other stories with historical settings they have read. Discuss how a story set in the past might differ from a contemporary story.

## Understand and apply reading strategies

- Read pp2–5 aloud, using appropriate expression. Discuss children's reactions to what they have heard. Encourage them to support their responses with reasons. How do they feel about Adewale being called Boy?
- Ask children to read pp6–11, looking for evidence of the historical setting. Take feedback from the activity.